My Pal Paul

by Louise Clayton
illustrated by Frank Sofo

Harcourt

Orlando   Boston   Dallas   Chicago   San Diego

Paul has been my neighbor since
we were babies. I don't remember
the first time I saw Paul, but I see
him every day now.

I have pictures of Paul and me
when we were babies. In this
photo, we are crawling around
on the lawn together.

I have pictures of Paul and
me when we were three. I like
the photo of us playing on the
seesaw the best.

I have pictures of Paul and me
when we were five. Look at us
sprawled out on the lawn! We're
tired after our game of tag.

Now Paul and I are ten. We
are still neighbors, and we are
still pals. Now we take pictures
of each other.

Sometimes I put my camera on automatic. Then we get pictures of Paul and me together! Here is one of us. Paul is yawning.

I like the picture of Paul and me
with my dog, Tawny. Her paws
are up in the air because she is
leaping up to catch the ball.

One morning at dawn, Paul
and I saw a deer with two fawns.
I got a great picture of Paul
looking at them.

Here is a picture Paul and I took
of a hawk. Paul taught me a lot
about hawks. He told me that
hawks have sharp claws.

Paul and I went on a flying-saucer
ride at the fair. Mom took a
picture. We look as if we are
being launched into space!

Maybe Paul and I will really be launched into space one day. We both want to be astronauts. Now we only pretend to be astronauts.

Paul likes to draw. He drew
a scarecrow that we had made
from straw. I took a photo of
his drawing.

Paul and I pick apples every
autumn. Then we make applesauce
from the fresh, raw apples.
Sometimes we make a mess, too.

I have pictures of Paul and me when
we were babies, when we were
three, and when we were five. I have
many pictures now that we are ten.

Maybe one day I will have
pictures of us launching into
space. For now, I am lucky
because Paul is a very good pal.